W9-BRI-395

FOLLOW THAT DOG!

Adapted by May Nakamura

Based on the episode written by Sarah Mullervy

Based on the TV show
Chico Bon Bon: Monkey with a Tool Belt

Ready-to-Read

Simon Spotlight
New York   London   Toronto   Sydney   New Delhi

SIMON SPOTLIGHT

An imprint of Simon & Schuster Children's Publishing Division
1230 Avenue of the Americas, New York, New York 10020
This Simon Spotlight edition December 2021
CHICO BON BON™ MONKEY WITH A TOOL BELT™ Chico Bon Bon: Monkey
with a Tool Belt Copyright © 2021 Monkey WTB Limited, a Silvergate Media
company. All rights reserved.
All rights reserved, including the right of reproduction in whole or in part
in any form. SIMON SPOTLIGHT, READY-TO-READ, and colophon are
registered trademarks of Simon & Schuster, Inc. For information about
special discounts for bulk purchases, please contact Simon & Schuster
Special Sales at 1-866-506-1949 or business@simonandschuster.com.
Manufactured in the United States of America 1021 LAK
2 4 6 8 10 9 7 5 3 1
ISBN 978-1-6659-0314-1 (hc)
ISBN 978-1-6659-0313-4 (pbk)
ISBN 978-1-6659-0315-8 (ebook)
33614082494369

Chico Bon Bon has a surprise for his friends.

He upgraded their old couch!

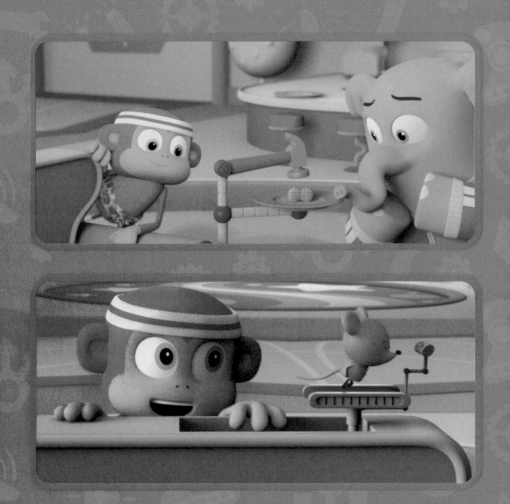

Now it has special features for Clark, Rainbow Thunder, Tiny, and Chico, too.

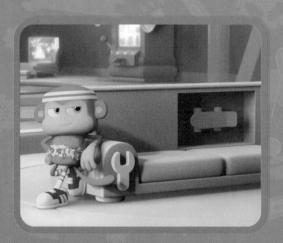

"This couch is now multi-functional!"
(say: MULL-tie-FUNK-shin-ul)
Chico says.

"Multi-what?" Clark asks.

"Multi means many.
A function is what
something does,"
Rainbow Thunder explains.

"Multifunctional means our couch can do many things!"

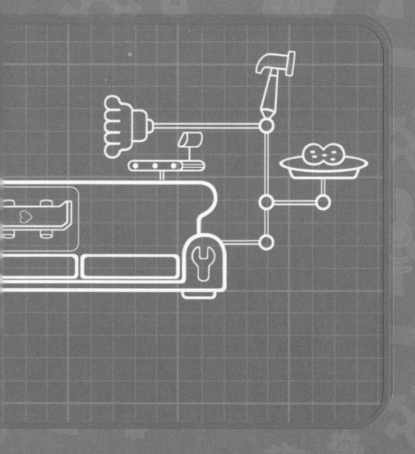

Ring! Ring!

It's the banana phone!

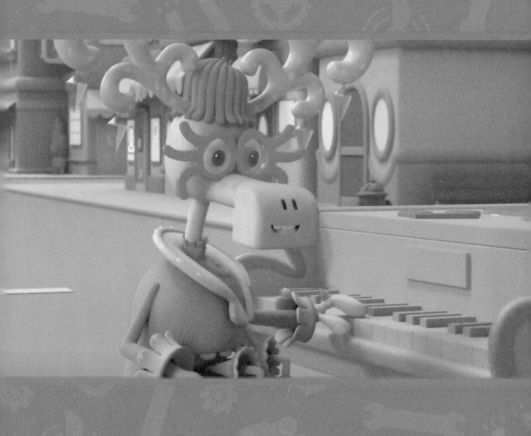

Elkin John, the famous singer, needs help!

His dog, Bernie, keeps
wiggling out of his leash.

Can the Fix-It Force
fix the problem?

The Fix-It Force and Bernie go on a walk.

Oh no!

Bernie wiggles loose!

They find Bernie
drinking water.
He is thirsty.

Rainbow Thunder suggests
a longer leash, but . . .

. . . Bernie wiggles loose again!

They find him
at a doggy day spa.
He wants a massage.

Clark suggests
a less slippery leash.
Chico builds one
out of rope.

Bernie wiggles loose again!
He wants to listen to some
cool music.

Oh no!
It is almost time for
Elkin John to return,
but nothing is working.

It is time to calm down
and take a banana break!

"Blazing bananas!"
Chico says. He has an idea!
"Maybe Bernie would not
wiggle out of his leash if it
had everything he likes."

Just like their
multifunctional couch,
Bernie needs
a multifunctional leash!

The Fix-It Force
snips and screws
a new leash together.

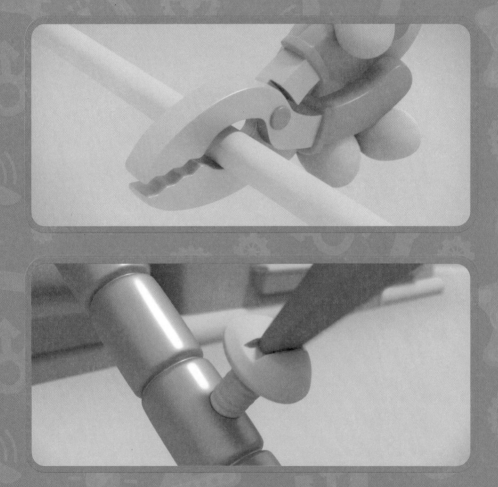

The leash has everything
Bernie wants!

It has a water cup,
plays cool music,
and massages his back.

It even has a doggy mike so he can sing along with Elkin!

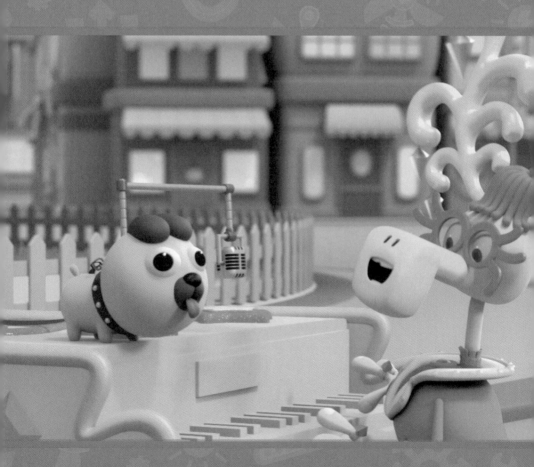

Now Bernie will never want to leave his leash again! "Thank you!" Elkin John says.

Science and teamwork save the day!

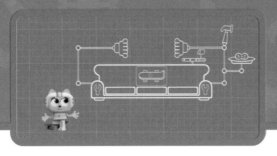

MULTIFUNCTIONAL OBJECTS ARE EVERYWHERE!

Just like the Fix-It Force's couch and Bernie's new leash, a **multifunctional** object is a gadget that can do many things.

Cell phones have many functions, like calling, texting, taking photos, and gaming. Cars have many functions, too, like driving, playing music, cooling, and heating.

But not all multifunctional objects are high-tech. Jackets keep you warm *and* carry things in their pockets. Some sofas can turn into beds, too. Can you think of any other examples? If you could invent any multifunctional object, what functions would it have?